J

The Best Vet in the World

Written by Charnan Simon • Illustrated by Carol Schwartz

Published in the United States of America by The Child's World®
PO Box 326 • Chanhassen, MN 55317-0326
800-599-READ • www.childsworld.com

Reading Adviser

Cecilia Minden-Cupp, PhD, Former Language and Literacy Program Director,
Harvard Graduate School of Education, Cambridge, Massachusetts

Acknowledgments

The Child's World®: Mary Berendes, Publishing Director

Editorial Directions, Inc.: E. Russell Primm, Editorial Director and Project Manager;
Katie Marsico, Associate Editor; Judith Shiffer, Assistant Editor; Caroline Wood, Editorial Assistant

The Design Lab: Kathleen Petelinsek, Design and Art Production

Library of Congress Cataloging-in-Publication Data

Simon, Charnan.
   The best vet in the world / written by Charnan Simon ; illustrated
by Carol Schwartz.
     p. cm. — (Magic door to learning)
   ISBN 1-59296-628-4 (library bound : alk. paper)
   1. Veterinarians—Juvenile literature. 2. Veterinary medicine—Juvenile literature.
  I. Schwartz, Carol, 1954–, ill. II. Title. III. Series.
 SF756.S556 2006
 636.089023—dc22   2006001632

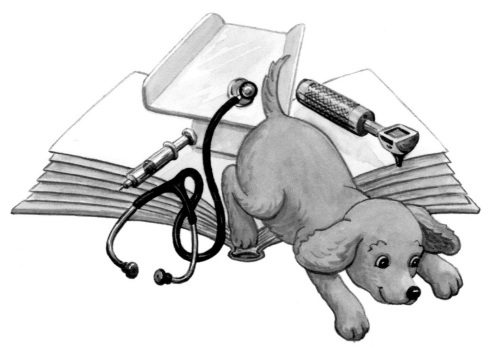

A book is a door, a magic door.
It can take you places
you have never been before.
Ready? Set?
Turn the page.
Open the door.
Now it is time to explore.

Our veterinarian is the
best vet in the world! We
met Dr. Linda when our
dog Sam was just a puppy.
Mom said all puppies
need a checkup from the
vet, just like babies need a
checkup from the doctor.

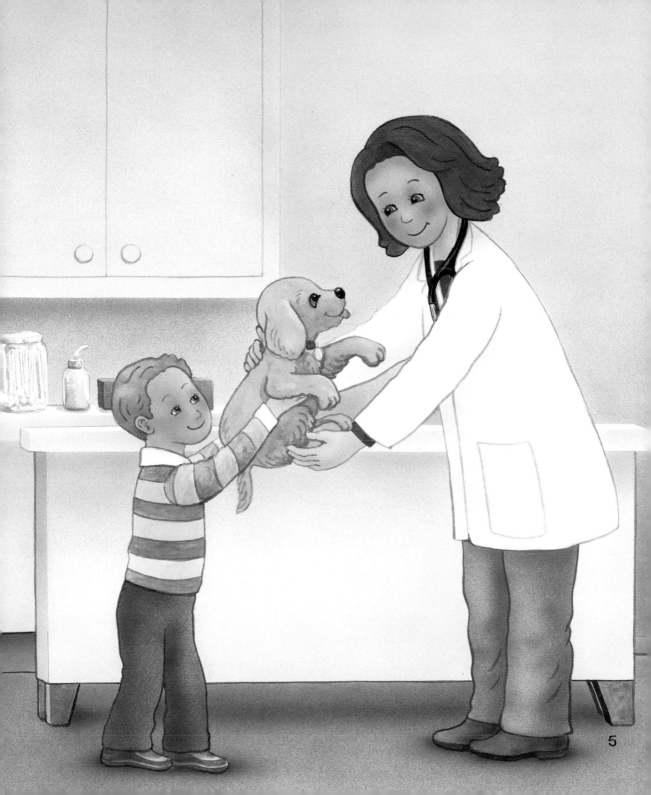

"Let's put Sam on the examining table,"
Dr. Linda said.

"What a happy, healthy-looking puppy!"

Dr. Linda looked at
Sam's skin and coat.
She listened to Sam's
heart and lungs.
"Good dog!" she said.

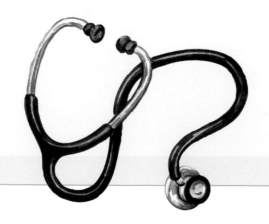

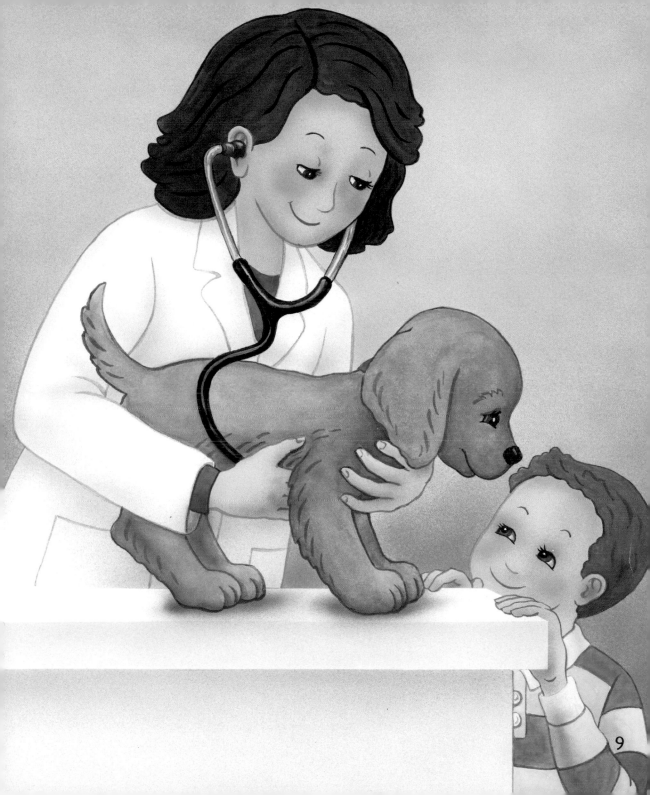

Dr. Linda felt Sam's tummy
and looked in his mouth.

She laughed when Sam tried to chew
her hand. "No biting," she said kindly.

Sam shook his head when
Dr. Linda looked in his ears.
"Does Sam scratch his ears
a lot?" she asked.
I nodded yes.
"Sam has ear mites,"
Dr. Linda said. "I'll give Sam
some medicine to make the
ear mites go away."

Next, Dr. Linda gave Sam a shot.
"Puppies need vaccinations,"
Dr. Linda explained.

14

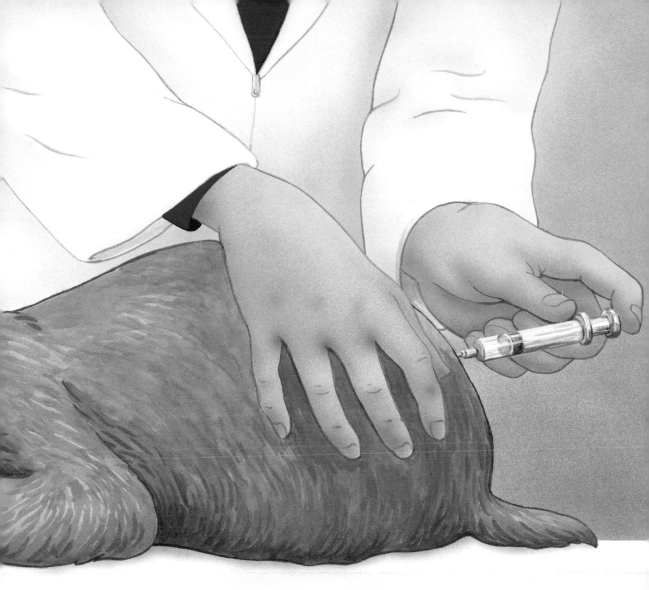

"Vaccinations help keep puppies from getting
diseases that could make them very sick."
"Ouch!" I said. Sam didn't seem to
mind at all.

15

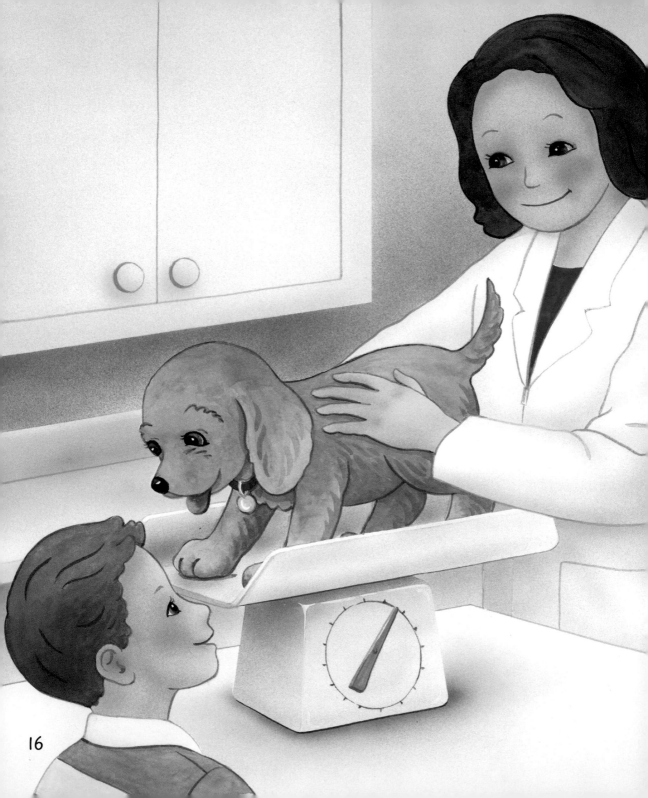

Dr. Linda put Sam on
the scale. "Twelve pounds!"
she said. "A perfect weight
for a puppy his age."

"Dr. Linda," I said.
"Your scale is little. What if
you had to weigh a pony?"

"I only treat small animals here,"
Dr. Linda said. "I take care of
animals such as cats, dogs, turtles,
birds, and gerbils."

18

"My friend Dr. Paul treats large animals in another office. He treats animals such as horses, cows, and ponies."

Dr. Linda patted Sam's head as she handed him to me. "Another friend, Dr. Susan, works at the zoo. She takes care of lions and tigers and giraffes!"

It would be exciting to take
care of animals in the zoo.
But I am glad Dr. Linda takes
care of small animals like Sam.

Sam is the best puppy in the world. And
Dr. Linda is the best vet in the world!

Our story is over, but there is still much to explore beyond the magic door!

Do you think you might want to be a vet? You can get good practice by studying where animals live, how they act, and what they eat. Have an adult help you find a place outdoors to lay out some birdseed and water. Pay attention to the animals that come and go. How do they act? How much do they eat? What do they look like? Be sure to write down some of your observations in a notebook. If you have time, draw pictures of the animals that you see.

These books will help you explore at the library and at home:

Boynton, Sandra. *My Puppy Book.* New York: Workman Publishers, 2005.

Huneck, Stephen. *Sally Goes to the Vet.* New York: Harry N. Abrams, 2004.

Lee, Spike, Tonya Lewis Lee, and Kadir Nelson (illustrator). *Please, Puppy, Please.* New York: Simon & Schuster for Young Readers, 2005.

About the Author

Charnan Simon lives in Madison, Wisconsin, where she can usually be found sitting at her desk and writing books, unless she is sitting at her desk and looking out the window. Charnan has one husband, two daughters, and two very helpful cats.

About the Illustrator

Carol Schwartz's award-winning illustrations have appeared in thirty-eight books for children. Having called Missouri and then Maryland home for many years, she now lives in Cincinnati, Ohio, with her husband.